WHY EXPLORE?

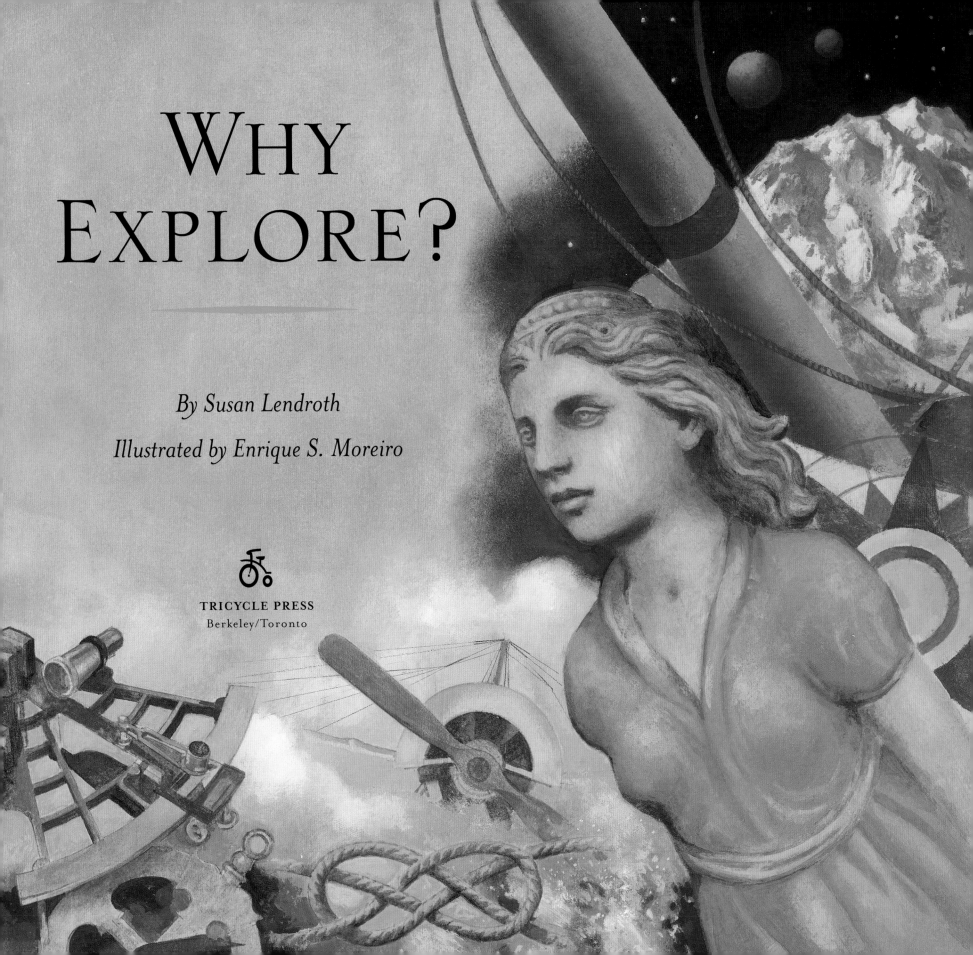

WHY EXPLORE?

By Susan Lendroth

Illustrated by Enrique S. Moreiro

TRICYCLE PRESS
Berkeley/Toronto

"Why explore?" the mother fondly said,
stroking the hair on her daughter's head.

"Other children stay close. Why must you roam?
Your place is with me, safe in our home."

"With a world so marvelous and wide,
I want to gather it all inside,
to learn the secrets of every creature,
to befriend the birds, make the woods my teacher."

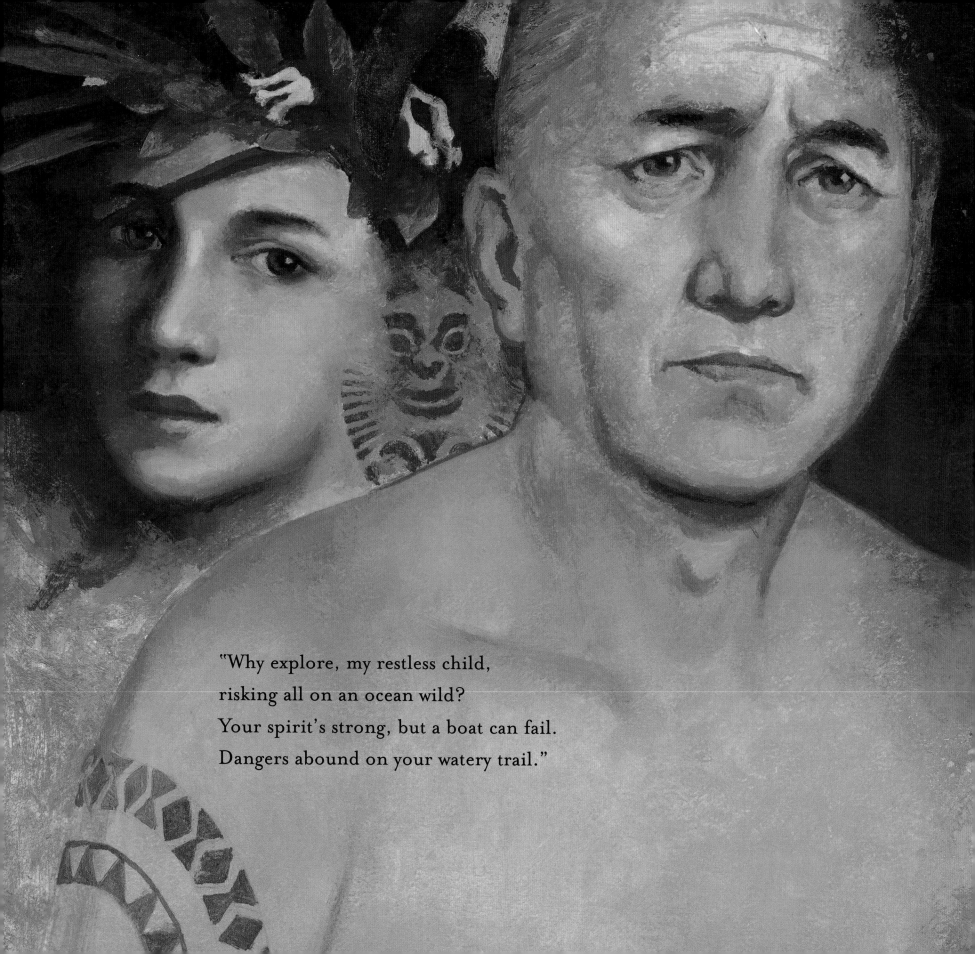

"Why explore, my restless child,
risking all on an ocean wild?
Your spirit's strong, but a boat can fail.
Dangers abound on your watery trail."

"Even paradise can grow too small
when you hear the far horizon's call.
Other lands await. Guides point the way—
the stars by night, the currents by day.

"Why explore?" the apprentice wondered.
"Into what sacred realms have we blundered?
It's sheer arrogance to try to render
an explanation for such splendor!"

"My goal is not some celestial tally,
counting the moon's every peak and valley,
but rather the heavenly sensation . . .

of further knowing this vast creation."

"Why explore," said the man to his wife,
"giving up this comfortable life?
We earn a good living making our soap,
while a sailor's lot is just rigging and rope!"

"'Tis not the ship," said his wife with a sigh.
"Our son's loved adventure since he was knee-high.
He follows his heart. It's the journey he craves—
the freedom, the peril, the wind, and the waves."

"Why explore, leaving family behind?
What can you possibly hope to find?
Sharecropping's not much, but we're settled here,
with all of our kinfolk gathered near."

"Ma, it's the kids, Eliza and John.
It's for their sake that we're moving on,
to homestead a farm and own some land,
where our children's children's home can stand."

"Why explore water scooped from a pond,
waving your pipette like a magic wand?
We can tell that it's not fit to drink
by the algae, the scum, the mud, and the stink."

"Ah, my young friend, it is not a mere puddle,
but a universe where millions huddle—
a microscopic dance on which we spy,
invisible to the unaided eye."

"Why explore old stuff dug from the ground?
Everything good has already been found.
All you have left are the rubbishy bits,
thrown long ago into ancient trash pits."

The archaeologist looked up from her pile.
"Even trash grows intriguing after a while.
Studying shards helps solve the mystery . . .

of vanished cultures throughout our history."

"Why explore a subatomic world
where energetic particles are hurled?
Please tell me, Professor, what's the use
of setting all those electrons loose?"

"Probing the building blocks of matter
involves more than making electrons scatter.
We are delving into the very heart
of how the universe got its start."

"Why explore?" the young boy cried.
"Sometimes those who've gone have died.
How can any adventure be worth
the risk of traveling far from Earth?"

"From the first person who gazed at the stars,
to mission teams planning trips to Mars,
an inner voice compels us to go—
to seek, discover, and, finally . . .

to know."

Author's Note

We humans are explorers at heart. We peer under rocks, walk down unknown paths, and travel to distant countries. Over the centuries, people have explored for many reasons, even creating inventions, from microscopes to spaceships, to reach new frontiers—as near as a drop of water, as far as a distant star.

POLYNESIAN NAVIGATORS

For over a thousand years the Polynesian navigators explored and helped settle the islands of the Pacific Ocean. They found their way across the sea in sturdy, well-built canoes without any of the modern instruments that sailors use today. Instead, they "read" the sea and sky. Stars orbit in a fixed pattern, and navigators used these patterns as a nighttime map to guide them. During the day, they studied the sun, clouds, seabirds, wind, and ocean currents.

Since our planet is round, Polynesian navigators were unable to see a distant island because it was below the horizon, hidden from view by the curve of the Earth. However, islands change the direction of the waves flowing around them. Master navigators could study the ocean carefully for these changes called "cross seas," which told them that land was near even if they couldn't see it. Navigators also followed the flight path of migratory seabirds and watched for the kind of high, stationary clouds that form over mountainous islands.

EARLY ASTRONOMY

Though he didn't invent the telescope, Galileo Galilei was the first person to turn one on the night sky and record what he saw there, in 1609. He saw the mountains of the moon and discovered that the planet Jupiter has moons of its own. Galileo wrote, "Saturn has ears!" when he saw a bulge on each side of the planet—early evidence of Saturn's rings. During Galileo's lifetime, religion influenced most aspects of life, including science and the law. He was ordered never to leave his home because he wrote in support of the idea that Earth and the other planets in our solar system orbit the sun. Catholic church teachings four hundred years ago claimed that the Earth was the center of the universe and everything else revolved around it. Galileo believed in God, but he also believed in what he saw with his own eyes: Earth *does* orbit the Sun.

VOYAGES OF EXPLORATION

During the eighteenth century, ships sailed from Europe to explore the far reaches of the globe. While many captains were primarily interested in finding new places to trade, some ships also carried naturalists on board who brought back information about exotic plants and unusual animals and birds. These explorers expanded the Western world's knowledge of distant lands. However, sometimes the discoveries were so unusual that people didn't believe they were real. When Australian colonists sent the first stuffed platypus to England, scientists thought it was a practical joke involving bits of different animals that had been sewn together. After all, who had ever heard of a creature that had a bill, webbed feet, and a furry body!

SHARECROPPERS AND HOMESTEADERS

In America after the Civil War, many poor Southern families turned to sharecropping to earn a living. Sharecroppers farmed land owned by someone else and paid rent on the land by sharing the crops, giving the landowner as much as 60 percent of the harvest. One way sharecroppers and other landless families could obtain their own farms was to travel west as homesteaders when the United States government offered settlers free land. Each homesteader could claim 160 acres to farm.

The property became theirs if they built a home, made improvements, and farmed it for five years. The journey west to find land was long, hard, and sometimes dangerous. While the Homestead Act of 1862 benefited many settlers by providing a way to own farms, often the Native Americans who originally lived in the area were forced to move to reservations.

MICROSCOPIC RESEARCH

Microscopes, first invented in the 1600s, opened a new realm to exploration—a very tiny, or microscopic, world that we cannot see with the naked eye. One of the first discoveries made with microscopes was that water taken from freshwater ponds teemed with life. To see this hidden world, a sample of water is drawn into a tube called a "pipette." A single drop of water from the pipette is then sandwiched between two glass slides and placed under the lens of the microscope. Life-forms with names like rotifer, hydra, and cyclops swim into magnified view. Microscopes have helped scientists research bacteria and viruses so that they can treat diseases.

ARCHAEOLOGY

Archaeologists explore the past through items made and used by people long ago. They are interested not only in grand finds like golden treasures, but also in everyday items such as cups, combs, and the bones left over from supper. Over time, buildings crumble and roads wash away. New cities are built on top of older ones. Archaeologists dig below the surface to find artifacts that help them study the ways of life in times past.

PARTICLE PHYSICS

Everything, from beach balls to bellybuttons, is made of matter. Anything with substance—anything that takes up any space at all—is matter. Scientists originally believed the smallest building blocks of matter were atoms, but we now know that atoms are made of still smaller pieces—subatomic particles such as protons, neutrons, and electrons. The best way for scientists to study subatomic particles like electrons is to smash atoms apart in giant accelerators, which force the particles to move very, very fast before they collide. For a brief moment after the collision, the subatomic particles separate. This enables scientists to explore what the universe was like at its beginning before atoms formed and eventually combined into stars and planets . . . and beach balls and bellybuttons.

SPACE EXPLORATION

Since Russian cosmonaut Yuri Gagarin first orbited Earth in 1961, over four hundred men and women have traveled into space. Some have lost their lives there. Space exploration can be dangerous, but astronauts rise to the challenge because they believe the rewards of journeying off our home planet are greater than the risks faced on the voyage.

After all, who knows what we may find beyond that most distant horizon?

Text copyright © 2005 by Susan Lendroth
Illustrations copyright © 2005 by Enrique S. Moreiro

TRICYCLE PRESS
a little division of Ten Speed Press
P.O. Box 7123
Berkeley, California 94707
www.tenspeed.com

Design by Susan Van Horn
Typeset in Mrs. Eaves and Serlio
The illustrations in this book were rendered in oil paint.

Library of Congress Cataloging-in-Publication Data

Lendroth, Susan.
 Why Explore? / by Susan Lendroth ; illustrated by Enrique Moreiro.
   p. cm.
 Summary: Rhyming text and illustrations present the human desire to
seek out the unknown and to learn as a result of it. Includes nonfiction
author's note.

 ISBN 1-58246-150-3

 [1. Explorers—Fiction. 2. Progress—Fiction. 3. Stories in rhyme.]

 I. Moreiro, Enrique S. (Enrique Sánchez), ill. II. Title.

 PZ8.3.L5397Wh 2005
 [Fic]—dc22
                 2004030088

First Tricycle Press printing, 2005
Printed in China

1 2 3 4 5 6 — 09 08 07 06 05